Lincolnshire
COUNTY COUNCIL

discover libraries

This book should be returned on or before the due date.

MC1

29/08/23

To renew or order library books please telephone 01522 782010
or visit https://lincolnshire.spydus.co.uk

You will require a Personal Identification Number.
Ask any member of staff for this.

The above does not apply to Reader's Group Collection Stock.

Bloomsbury Education
An imprint of Bloomsbury Publishing Plc

50 Bedford Square   1385 Broadway
London   New York
WC1B 3DP   NY 10018
UK   USA

www.bloomsbury.com

BLOOMSBURY and the Diana logo are trademarks of Bloomsbury Publishing Plc

First published in 2017 by Bloomsbury Education

A catalogue record for this book is available from the British Library.

ISBN: PB: 978-1-4729-3407-9
          ePub: 978-1-4729-3409-3
          ePDF: 978-1-4729-3406-2

2 4 6 8 10 9 7 5 3 1

Typeset by Integra Software Services Pvt. Ltd.

Printed in China by Leo Paper Products

MIX
Paper
FSC   FSC® C020056

This book is produced using paper that is made from wood grown in managed,
sustainable forests. It is natural, renewable and recyclable. The logging and manufacturing
processes conform to the environmental regulations of the country of origin.

To find out more about our authors and books visit www.bloomsbury.com.
Here you will find extracts, author interviews, details of forthcoming
events and the option to sign up for our newsletters.

recommended by

www.catchup.org

Catch Up is a charity which aims to address the problem of underachievement that
has its roots in literacy and numeracy difficulties.

ALL TOO MUCH

JO COTTERILL

ILLUSTRATED BY
MARIA GARCIA BORREGO

BLOOMSBURY EDUCATION
AN IMPRINT OF BLOOMSBURY

LONDON OXFORD NEW YORK NEW DELHI SYDNEY

CONTENTS

Chapter One

Samira turned to her friend Hani and smiled.

"We did it!" she said. "We won the debate."

Samira and Hani were in the school debating club.

The debate had been about school uniform. Samira and Hani were arguing that pupils should not be made to wear a uniform.

Hani high-fived her. "You mean **you** did it. I don't know how you think that fast! Your answers were just awesome."

"The funny thing is," said Samira, "I actually think school uniform **is** a good idea!"

"You know so much about so many things," Hani said, as they left the classroom. "You never stop reading. How do you fit all that stuff in your head?"

"I just find lots of things interesting," said Samira. "And education is so important. I want to learn as much as I can. Isn't that why we are here?"

"I suppose so..." Hani said, but she didn't sound sure. Samira was not exactly a typical student at Hopewell High. It was a posh private girls' boarding school and you had to pass an exam to get in. Hani worked hard at her lessons but she liked to have fun too.

Just then Samira heard someone calling her name. It was Mr Portman, their year tutor.

"See you back at the Nest," Hani said to Samira. The Nest was the bedroom she and Samira shared with two other girls.

Samira tucked a strand of hair back under her hijab and went over to Mr Portman.

He was a tall, skinny man who always looked untidy, but he was a kind teacher and good at listening. "Your father rang this morning," Mr Portman said.

Samira felt anxious. "It's not even Friday!" she said. Her father liked to know exactly how she was getting on at school. He rang for a progress report every Friday, but today was only Wednesday.

"He wanted to know how you did in the French test yesterday," Mr Portman said.

Samira looked down for a moment. "I got sixteen out of twenty." It was lower than her usual mark. Her father was bound to ask why she hadn't done better. She did not have a good answer. She just hadn't learned the vocab well enough. Her father would not be pleased. Her head felt fuzzy, like it was full of grey mist.

Mr Portman looked at Samira. Then he said, "I'm a bit worried about you. You're putting yourself under so much pressure. Are you coping?"

Samira looked up in alarm. "Of course I am! I'm fine!"

"Don't forget," said Mr Portman, "that life isn't just about work. You must take a break sometimes. Have fun."

Fun? Samira almost laughed. School wasn't about having fun. It was about learning! That was why her parents had sent her here when she was eleven, all the way from her home in Iran. In Iran everyone knew how important a good education was. But here in England, some of the girls didn't seem to care if they did well or not. She made herself smile. "I do take breaks," she said. "And I have fun with my friends."

Mr Portman smiled back. "I'm glad to hear it. I'll tell your father that the French result is not in yet." He winked.

"Thanks," Samira said. She knew her father would simply ring again the next day to find out how she did, but it was kind of Mr Portman to cover for her.

And it was not all a lie. She **did** have fun with her friends. And now that lessons were finished for the day, it was time to meet up with them!

Chapter Two

Samira shared The Nest with her three best friends: Alice, Hani and Daisy. The four of them were very different but they loved hanging out together.

The Nest wasn't the biggest dormitory – it could just about fit in four beds, four wardrobes, and four desks – but it was at the opposite end of the corridor from the house mistress, Miss Redmond. It was very important to be far away from the house mistress if you were planning a midnight feast!

There were six flights of stairs to get to the Nest, and Samira felt much better about things as she reached the top. Her friends would cheer her up. But as she got near to the door, she could hear loud voices arguing. Samira gave a sigh. Not again! She knew exactly who it was – Alice and Daisy.

"It was right here on my desk," Daisy was saying.

"Well, I didn't take it," Alice said.

"If you didn't, who did? Hani and Samira don't even wear make-up!" Daisy turned as Samira came into the room. "Samira, have you seen my mascara? The brand new one, in the blue tube?"

Samira shook her head. "Sorry."

"I neeeeed it!" Daisy wailed. Her thick dark hair was curled at the bottom, which looked natural but took half an hour to get right. "I'm going into town to see Blaze!"

Alice laughed. "That's **so** not his name. Tell me that's not his name!"

Daisy glared at her. "It is too. He's totally hot."

Hani was lying on her bed, reading a magazine. "You can't go into town," she pointed out. "You're not allowed on your own."

"I know that," Daisy said. "One of you will come with me. Won't you?" She made her blue-green eyes go big. Even without mascara, Daisy was still gorgeous.

Hani laughed but Samira shook her head. "What about your homework? Have you done your English for tomorrow?" she asked.

Daisy waved a hand like she didn't care. "Oh, I'll throw something together later."

Samira bit her lip. She never understood Daisy's attitude. How could meeting a boy be more important than her homework?

Alice gave a sigh. "I'll come into town with you." She put down the pictures she had cut from her magazine. She was sticking them onto her wardrobe door. They were all pictures of film stars. "And you can borrow my mascara, OK?"

Daisy smiled at her. "You're a superstar. For real. When you're famous in Hollywood, I'll be able to say, 'I borrowed her mascara once.'"

Alice and Daisy were best friends half the time – and the other half they spent arguing.

Sometimes they didn't talk to each other for days – and then they were besties all over again. Samira and Hani had got used to it.

Samira sat down at her desk. She had so much to do. She had done her English homework days ago, but maybe she should check it again. If she didn't get a good mark, she would be letting herself down. And her family back home.

And, she remembered, she should talk to the French teacher. She needed to take the test again, to see if she could do better. Her father would expect it.

Samira looked at the framed photo on her desk – a photo of Malala, the girl from Pakistan who was the youngest-ever winner of the Nobel Peace Prize. Malala knew the real value of education. She was Samira's hero, so Samira had a lot to live up to.

While her friends chatted about boys and parties and texting, Samira started work.

Chapter Three

It was two days later that Mr Portman called
Samira over for another chat. She felt dizzy.
Had her father found out about the bad mark in
the French test? But Mr Portman was smiling.

"Are you up for a new challenge, Samira? Something fun, I hope."

"Er..." said Samira.

"Miss Okoro and I are in charge of the Hopewell High quiz team," began Mr Portman.

Samira frowned. Every year the school entered a national quiz competition. The team members were always aged between sixteen and eighteen. What did this have to do with her? She was only fourteen!

"Someone has dropped out," Mr Portman went on. "And with all the reading you do, we think you're the ideal person to step in. We would like to offer you a place on the team."

Samira stared at him. "Me? Are you sure?"

He nodded. "You know a lot about geography, politics and history. Probably more than the older girls. We think you would be great on the team. But I don't want to add to your stress. The quiz is supposed to be fun. It's a chance to show everyone how much you already know. What do you think?"

Samira gulped. It was a big honour to be asked. Her father would be so proud of her. She felt she could not say no. "Thank you, Mr Portman. I would love to."

Mr Portman smiled. "Come along after lessons on Monday for a practice."

Samira worked hard all evening, even though it was Friday. The others went off to play games in the common room and drink hot chocolate while watching a film – the usual Friday–evening activity. Hani tried to get Samira to come along too. "You're allowed one evening off," she said.

Samira thought about it. The film sounded like a good one. She did usually go… and it was always so nice, just to have a couple of hours off from studying. "I've been picked for the school quiz team," she told Hani.

"The quiz team?" Hani said. She sounded surprised. "But you're not old enough."

"Someone dropped out and Mr Portman asked me to take her place." Samira couldn't help feeling proud.

Hani gave a great whoop and threw her arms around her friend. "That's AMAZING!! You must be the youngest person on the team ever! Come on, you HAVE to come and celebrate now. No excuses."

Samira laughed. "I can't. Honestly. Next week, I'll come. But I want to start preparing for the quiz."

Hani shook her head. "You are **hopeless**." But she was smiling when she said it. "All right, see you later."

Samira smiled back. "Have a good time." But her smile faded as soon as the Nest was empty. That was happening more and more – putting on a smile when she didn't feel like it. The truth was, deep down, the idea of being on the quiz team terrified her. What if she got a question wrong in front of everyone? What if the school lost because of her?

Mr Portman had said the quiz was supposed to be fun, but she knew she should do some extra reading to prepare.

Samira stared at the desk in front of her. Her laptop was open, showing a news page. Her history and chemistry textbooks lay next to it. There was so much to do... Where should she even start? She was a clever girl, everyone said so. Everyone (especially her father) expected so much of her.

But sometimes, just sometimes, Samira wished it would all just go away. Why couldn't she go and have fun, like the others? Why did she always have to work? But if she didn't work, she would only worry about it...

Her head felt full of thick grey mist again. The words on the screen blurred in front of her eyes. She couldn't concentrate. She needed to do something to clear her mind.

Only one thing helped at a time like this. Samira got up and checked that there was no one in the corridor outside. Then she came back into the Nest and shut the door. She pulled up her sleeve. One advantage of always wearing long sleeves was that no one saw your arms...

Ten minutes later, her head felt clearer, and she got back to work.

Chapter Four

Mr Portman and Miss Okoro were setting up the questions when Samira arrived for the quiz practice on Monday.

There were four of them on the quiz team. Keris was eighteen, tall with blonde hair and a friendly smile. Poon was eighteen too, from Thailand. Poon was really good at history, although she was not very good at any other type of question. Precious was sixteen and very glad to see Samira. "I don't know why they asked me," she whispered to Samira. "I hardly know anything!"

This turned out to be untrue. Precious could answer loads of questions. She knew who the French prime minister was. She knew the name of the longest river in South America.

She even knew the top three most venomous snakes in the world. She kept turning to Samira with a look of surprise and saying, "I can't believe I knew the answer to that one!"

Mr Portman and Miss Okoro were pleased with Samira, but she felt she could have done better. "I **knew** it was Homer who wrote 'The Odyssey'," she said, after giving the wrong answer. "I'm so sorry! I don't know why I couldn't remember!"

"Hey," said Keris, "it's OK. Don't beat yourself up about it."

But Samira was annoyed with herself. Later, when she was back in the tutor room doing her homework, Hani tried to calm her down. "Look," she said, "it was just a practice."

"But I have to be able to think faster!" exclaimed Samira. "I can't get easy ones like that wrong! And I **knew** it!"

Hani sighed. "Sammy, don't you think you're over-reacting? Nobody's perfect, you know. It's OK to get things wrong sometimes."

"Not me," said Samira firmly. "It's OK for other people to get things wrong, but not me."

"But not everyone is top of their game all the time," Hani said. "I know how good I am at running, but do I hit my top speed every time? Of course not! Some days, you're just not quite as good as other days."

Samira looked down. "What if I'm not having a good day on the day of the quiz? What if I let everyone down?"

"You won't," Hani said. She reached out and put a hand on Samira's arm to comfort her, but Samira quickly pulled her arm away.

"What's the matter?" Hani asked. "Have you hurt yourself?"

Samira felt cold at Hani's words. "Have you hurt yourself?" What would Hani say if she knew the truth? "I'm fine," Samira said in a sharp voice.

"Girls," Miss Redmond called from the front of the room. "No talking, please."

Samira didn't look at her friend as she opened her history textbook. But a moment later, Hani slid a note across the desk.

"We're called 'friends' for a reason. If there's something going on, I can help."

Samira stared at it, feeling tears sting her eyes. She blinked them back. No. No one could help. This was something she had to sort out on her own. She scribbled "I'm fine" on the note and slid it back.

Hani read, it, looked at Samira and then got on with her work. Samira felt disappointed and relieved all at once.

As the day of the quiz came nearer, Samira found it harder and harder to sleep at night. There seemed to be so much to do! Her father now emailed her every day with links to useful websites, so that she could read as much as possible for the quiz.

There might be a question on how rice was grown. Or Indian gods. Or the kings and queens of England... She couldn't tell her friends how tired she was, or how unhappy she felt. She was Samira! Everyone knew she was clever and top of the class. Everyone knew things came easily to her... How could she let them know that she was sinking?

Under her sleeves, Samira's arms stung. Her secret was the only thing helping her get through every day.

Chapter Five

It was bedtime on a Monday and Samira was in the Nest with the others. She had been to another quiz practice and was angry with herself for getting three questions wrong.

The competition was only three days away; she couldn't afford to make mistakes.

All four of the friends were getting changed for bed. Daisy had dumped Blaze and was now chatting up another boy online. "It's so risky," Alice said, watching Daisy send a flirty message on her phone. "You don't know who he is really. He could be some dirty old man who has stolen a photo of a fit lad."

Daisy laughed. "I'm not so stupid as to message a stranger. My friend Becca from home knows him. He's called Storm."

"**Storm**?" Hani raised her eyebrows. "What is it with you and boys with weird names?" she asked.

"Yeah?" Daisy snapped back. "No weirder than Hani."

Hani looked hurt. "It's Ethiopian; you know that. After my gran." She turned away from Daisy and looked across at Samira. "Just because it's foreign doesn't mean..." Then she saw Samira's arm and her words stopped dead.

Samira felt herself go cold all over. She hadn't put her pyjama top on quickly enough. Her arm was uncovered.

"What the... what's **that**?" whispered Hani.

Samira didn't need to look at her arm for the answer. She knew what was there: a pattern of straight lines cut into the skin, some fresh and red, some old and silvery.

Everyone was quiet. Samira couldn't look up. She just kept staring at the carpet. She heard Daisy swear, and then Alice said, quietly, "Sammy... have you been... cutting yourself?"

What could she say? She nodded.

"But why?" Hani asked. "Everything is going so well!"

"No, it isn't," Samira whispered. "I'm not good enough. I'm letting everyone down."

Alice came over to sit on Samira's bed. Samira pulled her pyjama top on quickly, covering her arm again. "Why would you think that? You always come top of the class."

Samira shook her head. "I should be doing better."

"Well, you won't do better by doing **that** to yourself." Daisy's voice was shocked. "What the hell were you thinking? That's just... just... **sick**."

"Daisy, that's harsh," Alice said sharply.

Samira began to tremble. "I didn't... I didn't know what else to do."

Hani looked at her. "Why didn't you tell us? Sammy, we are your **friends**."

"I'm sorry," Samira whispered.

"You have to go and tell Miss Redmond," Alice said. Their house mistress was strict but she was good at listening. Last year, she had needed to sort out Alice and Daisy's arguments almost every week.

Samira was horrified. "I can't! She would tell my father! And then..." She couldn't even bear to think what might happen if he knew.

"It's not the work that's the problem," said Daisy harshly, "it's your head. No one in their right mind would cut their own arms. I'm going to the bathroom. I can't look at you." The door slammed behind her.

Samira burst into tears. Hani and Alice tried to comfort her. "We'll help you. Just tell us what's going on, Sammy."

"I can't cope," sobbed Samira. "If I didn't have the quiz, on top of everything else..."

"Well, that's something we **can** fix," Alice said.

Samira wiped her eyes. "I can't quit."

Alice grinned at her. "You don't have to. We can fix it so that the quiz never takes place."

There was a pause.

"What do you mean?" asked Samira, staring at her.

"Remember when we first came here? What happened in our very first week?" Alice looked full of mischief. "**Everyone** was talking about it."

Hani's brown eyes were wide with horror. "You're not thinking what I think you're thinking...?" She groaned. "You **are**! Alice, the last time anyone tried that they nearly burned down the school!"

Chapter Six

When Alice explained the plan, Samira was so shocked she stopped crying. "We can't do that! We will get into so much trouble! Someone got expelled last time, didn't they?"

"Of course not!" Alice scoffed. "They were suspended for a week, that's all."

"That does **not** make it OK!" Hani said.

Alice grinned. "No one will know it was us. Seriously – it's a brilliant idea. And with your science brain…"

"I've never tried to make a stink bomb before," Samira told her firmly. "It's not exactly part of the science curriculum."

"But you could do it," Alice insisted. "Look it up on the internet; I bet there are loads of videos. And then the quiz won't happen because the smell in the hall will be so disgusting it will have to be cancelled!"

Hani nodded slowly. "I hate to say it, but it's a good plan. As long as we get the mixture right. Last time, the chemicals somehow caught fire. I think the girl left it on a radiator – a stupid thing to do."

Samira shook her head. "We can't do this. I don't want to get you into trouble. I'll just..." She took a deep breath. "I'll just have to stop hurting myself. It's ridiculous. I don't know why I do it." Then she burst into tears again. Hani put her arm around her friend.

"Look," said Alice, "you can trust us. Remember when I started getting panic attacks last year? You guys helped me through it. Let us help you. The first thing we need to do is get the quiz cancelled. And this is the only way to do it."

*　*　*

It was the morning of the quiz, and students from nine other schools were due in just half an hour. Alice and Samira met outside the school hall.

"I can't believe we're doing this," Samira whispered. She passed Alice a glass jam jar. "It's all in there. You just have to take the lid off – and run. Where are you going to put it?"

Alice grinned. "Somewhere they'll never find it – not until it's too late." She took the jar, her sleeves pulled down over her hands. "Got to rub it down so there's no fingerprints. I've learned a lot from breaking rules with Daisy!"

Samira bit her lip. Daisy had not spoken to her since Monday evening. Samira hated that they were not friends any more. She wished Daisy understood what she was going through. But how could she, when Samira was not really sure herself?

"See you later," Alice said, and stepped into the hall.

When the other teams arrived for the quiz, Mr Portman showed everyone into the hall. Samira held her breath, knowing what to expect. Within seconds, over sixty people were running for the exits, holding their noses.

"Ugh! What is that stink?!" exclaimed a tall dark-haired boy. "It smells like something has **died** in there. I think I'm going to be sick."

"We can't hold the quiz in there," one of the visiting teachers told Mr Portman.

It was working! Samira pressed her lips together to stop a smile. She wouldn't have to compete!

By now quite a crowd of girls from Hopewell High had gathered, staring at the visitors who filled the corridor, coughing and spluttering.

The tall boy sniffed again and frowned. "That's... hang on, that smells like... a **stink bomb**!"

Samira felt her stomach flip. Oh no! She was going to be found out!

"Don't be silly," his teacher said. "It must be a problem with the toilets."

"No," the boy insisted, "no, it's not. I should know, I've made one myself!" He grabbed his teacher's arm. "Listen to me! Someone is playing a joke! It's..."

"STORM?" someone suddenly shouted.

Samira swung round. Standing in the middle of the corridor, looking totally amazed, was Daisy.

"DAISY?" said the boy.

"I can't believe it!" she squealed. "What are **you** doing here?"

Chapter Seven

To the surprise of everyone watching, Daisy threw herself into Storm's arms. "I never thought we would actually get to meet!"

He hugged her back. "I didn't know you were at this school!"

There was such a fuss and noise that Storm's mention of a stink bomb was completely forgotten. The quiz was cancelled and everyone just went into the canteen for tea. All the very serious, clever students became very silly, stuffing themselves with cake and biscuits and giggling about how they had nearly puked everywhere. Even the teachers seemed to enjoy themselves.

"We will have to fix another date for the quiz," Samira heard Mr Portman say to one of the visitors. "It's so difficult finding a date that everyone can do."

"Some people seem to find a date easily," the teacher replied. She pointed across the room at Daisy and Storm, who were sitting together at a table gazing into each other's eyes.

"Mr Portman," Samira said quietly, "can I talk to you?"

"Yes, of course." He moved to a quiet corner of the room with her. "What is it?"

Samira bit her lip. She didn't want to tell Mr Portman how she was feeling. He might be disappointed in her and she would hate that.

"The thing is..." she said, "I'm not coping very well, and I think being on the quiz team is too much pressure for me. I think it would be better if I didn't take part."

Mr Portman looked at her for a moment and then smiled. "Of course, Samira. I know you push yourself very hard. It's important you recognise when you've got too much on. Good for you."

Samira's legs felt wobbly with relief. "You're not disappointed in me?"

"No, of course I'm not, and I'll make sure your father understands that too," said Mr Portman.

It was as if he had read her mind! "Thank you," said Samira softly.

* * *

"See?" said Hani, when they were back in the Nest that evening. "It's not as awful as you think."

"You made it a bigger thing in your mind than it really was," Alice added. "That's what happens to me when I have a panic attack. Your mind plays tricks on you."

"Thanks, both of you," Samira said. "I should have told you earlier about... what I'd been doing. I do feel better."

The door opened and the three of them looked up to see Daisy. Samira felt nervous. Was Daisy about to have another go at her?

But Daisy had the biggest smile on her face ever. "This has been the best day of my life," she announced. "I am **totally** in love!" She bounced over to Samira's bed. "And it's all thanks to you!" She gave Samira an enormous hug.

Samira hugged her back, surprised. "You're not – you don't hate me?"

"Hate you?" Daisy pulled back. "Don't be silly. I don't get what you've been doing at all – I mean, hurting yourself on purpose just seems completely off the planet to me. But I think I went a bit over the top."

"Only a bit?" Hani teased her.

Daisy aimed a punch at Hani's shoulder. "Shut up. I'm trying to say sorry, OK? I can't be mad at **anyone** right now because I'm soooo in love!" She flopped back on Hani's bed opposite. "Can I tell you everything? I'm bursting! He's so adorable!"

The other three smiled at each other as Daisy started a list of Storm's attractive qualities. "Storm and Daisy sounds all wrong," Alice whispered. "Maybe she should change her name to Lightning." The other two giggled.

"You OK?" Hani asked Samira quietly.

Samira shook her head. "Not yet. I mean, there's still so much stuff in my mind. But talking about it really helps. I think maybe I should talk to someone else, too. I might try Miss Redmond."

"She would be cool, I think," Hani said. "She was good with Alice and Daisy last year."

"Yeah." Samira looked round as Daisy carried on talking about Storm. She was lucky to have such good friends. They might have their ups and downs, but they were always there for each other.

"Thanks, Hani," she said. And this time her smile was a real one.

Bonus Bits!

GUESS WHO?

Each piece of information below is about one of these people in the story:

1 Samira

2 Hani

3 Alice

4 Daisy

5 Mr Portman

6 Miss Redmond

7 Miss Okoro

8 Keris

9 Poon

10 Precious

Match each person to a piece of information by writing the right letter next to the right number on a sheet of paper. Check your answers at the end of this section (no peeking!).

A Her grandmother is Ethiopian.

B She falls in love with Storm.

C She was born in Iran.

D She was jointly in charge of the quiz team.

E She is 18 and from Thailand.

F She is a house mistress.

G She is 18 and has blonde hair.

H He is skinny and tall.

I She knew the name of the French prime minister.

J She sometimes has panic attacks.

WHAT IS A HIJAB?

In the story, Samira is wearing a hijab. But what is a hijab?

A hijab is a type of scarf or veil traditionally worn by Muslim women and girls in the presence of adult men who are not in their family (e.g. male teachers in this story). It covers the head and neck, leaving the face visible but covering up the hair. It is a symbol of modesty and privacy.

WHO IS MALALA?

Malala is mentioned in the book. Here is a little more information about her.

- Malala Yousafzai is a Pakistani activist for female education. She is the youngest-ever winner of the Nobel Peace Prize.

- In 2009, when she was 11 to 12 years old, Malala wrote a blog about her life under Taliban occupation. The Taliban did not allow girls to have education. She became more outspoken and shared her views more widely.

- In October 2012, Malala was on a school bus. A gunman asked for her by name and then shot her three times. A few days later she was flown to Queen Elizabeth Hospital in Birmingham and recovered from the attack.

- From March 2013 Malala was a pupil at an all-girls school in Birmingham. She has kept fighting for all women and girls to be allowed to be educated.

WHERE TO GET HELP

Samira feels a huge amount of pressure from her family as well as the pressure she places on herself. She can't cope with this alone and doesn't share her feelings, and this means that she takes extreme measures.

If you have concerns and worries about things, there are people outside of your immediate family and friends who can help.

Childline

Childline is a free, 24-hour counselling service for everyone under 18. Childline says, "You can talk to us about anything. No problem is too big or too small. We're on the phone and online. However you choose to contact us, you're in control. It's free, confidential and you don't have to give your name if you don't want to."

www.childline.org.uk / telephone: 0800 1111

Mind

Mind is a charity for people with mental health problems. It can provide help and information if you or someone you know is self-harming like Samira. It is for adults and children.

www.mind.org.uk / telephone: 0300 123 3393 / text: 86463

WHAT NEXT?

- Why do you think Samira put so much pressure on herself?
- How could Samira have coped with the pressure she felt in a better way?
- Why are friends important?

If you enjoyed reading this story and haven't already read *Hopewell High – Stage Fright*, grab yourself a copy and curl up somewhere to read it!

ANSWERS to GUESS WHO?
1c 2a 3j 4b 5h 6f 7d 8g 9e 10i

LOOK OUT FOR MORE ADVENTURES FROM HOPEWELL HIGH!

ISBN 978 1 4729 3413 0